Samuel French Acting Edition

Long Way Go Down

by Zayd Dohrn

I0589041

SAMUEL FRENCH

SAMUELFRENCH.COM   SAMUELFRENCH.CO.UK

FOR PRODUCTION ENQUIRIES

UNITED STATES AND CANADA
Info@SamuelFrench.com
1-866-598-8449
UNITED KINGDOM AND EUROPE
Plays@SamuelFrench.co.uk
020-7255-4302

Each title is subject to availability from Samuel French, depending upon country of performance. Please be aware that *LONG WAY GO DOWN* may not be licensed by Samuel French in your territory. Professional and amateur producers should contact the nearest Samuel French office or licensing partner to verify availability.

MUSIC USE NOTE

Licensees are solely responsible for obtaining formal written permission from copyright owners to use copyrighted music in the performance of this play and are strongly cautioned to do so. If no such permission is obtained by the licensee, then the licensee must use only original music that the licensee owns and controls. Licensees are solely responsible and liable for all music clearances and shall indemnify the copyright owners of the play(s) and their licensing agent, Samuel French, against any costs, expenses, losses and liabilities arising from the use of music by licensees. Please contact the appropriate music licensing authority in your territory for the rights to any incidental music.

IMPORTANT BILLING AND CREDIT REQUIREMENTS

If you have obtained performance rights to this title, please refer to your licensing agreement for important billing and credit requirements.

LONG WAY GO DOWN was first produced by Kitchen Dog Theater in Dallas, Texas in 2010. The performance was directed by Chris Carlos, with sets by Bryan Wofford, costumes by Tina Parker, lights by Linda Blase, music and sound by John M. Flores, and fight choreography by Bill Lengfelder and Cameron Cobb. The cast was as follows:

BILLY. . . . . Bruce DuBose

CHRIS . . . . Drew Wall

NINI. . . . . .Ivan Jasso

VIOLETTA. . . . . Ani Celise Vera

CHARACTERS

BILLY – forties, an American trucker
CHRIS – twenties, his son
NINI & **VIOLETTA** – twenties, two undocumented immigrants
The **TIRED VOICE** of an older woman

SETTING

An apartment building; a public phone; a safe house outside of
Phoenix; the cab of a semi truck; the desert

TIME

Present

Scene One

(A safe house, doubling as a truck dispatch office, near the Mexican/American border. The walls are falling apart, and half of the area is sectioned off with clear plastic sheets hung from the ceiling.)

(The small space left over contains a desk, two chairs, a promotional calendar, and an old CB radio.)

*(**CHRIS**, twenties, stands on tiptoe on the desk, hanging a piece of plastic with a staple gun.)*

*(His father, **BILLY**, forties, helps him.)*

*(**VIOLETTA**, twenties, sits off to the side, wearing a floral-print dress and cheap high-heels, watching them.)*

BILLY. So, spring break…

CHRIS. Right?

BILLY. College white boys. *Girls Gone Wild.*

CHRIS. *Nice.* With the cameras, Pop?

BILLY. Cameras are there. Bunch of coeds, down from campus. UCSC. Santa Cruz. All dolled up, y'know –

(Showing his nipples.)

"TJ! Yaaaahhh!"

CHRIS. *(Laughs.)* Yeah.

BILLY. Having a wild time. Jell-O shots are there. Mud wrestling is there.

CHRIS. Awesome.

BILLY. And all the locals are watching – "This how gringos behave? Amazing!"

CHRIS. Happy to see that cash though.

BILLY. To a point, maybe, but – Anyway, this one guy, Mickey, I was telling you about? My partner there? He's out walking his family one evening. And this frat boy from Texas is sitting on the curb. Baseball cap. Board shorts. Lost his friends, got kicked out of a club, whatever. And he says something to Mickey's wife.

CHRIS. What's he say?

BILLY. Something, I don't know.

CHRIS. Something bad?

BILLY. Whatever people say, Chris, you know. I wasn't there. He speaks to her. Makes a gesture.

CHRIS. In front of her husband?

BILLY. Well…Mickey's like four-foot-nine, ten, right? Tiny little man. This kid's a linebacker from UT or something.

CHRIS. Okay.

BILLY. So Mickey smiles, like – "Gracias, Amigo… No comprende inglés… No comprende… U.S.A… Walt Disney World!" Takes his wife and kid home, goes into his shed, takes out his ball-peen hammer –

CHRIS. Uh-oh.

BILLY. – And heads back into town, right. Finds the kid passed out on the sidewalk. Big fat smile on his face, hugging a beef burrito to his chest like it's a teddy bear. So Mickey grabs his hair –

*(He demonstrates on **CHRIS**.)*

Pulls his head back, opens his mouth, takes the hammer, and WHAM!

CHRIS. Get off me, man –

BILLY. – Breaks off his front teeth. Kid wakes up, eyes bugging out, teeth in the back of his throat, tries to stand. But Mickey's got a boot on his neck now. Holds his mouth open, and smashes the bottom teeth. And the guy starts bawling –

(He imitates the guy crying with no teeth.)

"Luhh… Luhh…" And Mickey's trying to get the side teeth out too, like "Wham! Wham! Wham!" But it's hard, apparently, to get those side teeth out with a hammer, right? He keeps hitting the kid's cheeks by accident. And a crowd starts to gather, but nobody's helping. TJ police just stand there, half-asleep, "'nother fucking Yankee getting his face worked on. Pobrecito. What else is new?" And the guy is puking day-glo blue from all the "Hpnotiq" liquor they have in the clubs there. Pieces of his teeth sticking through his lips like onion in a hamburger. And finally Mickey pockets the hammer, unzips his pants, and goes "¡Quién es el mamá huevos ahora, pinche gringo!"

> (**BILLY** *laughs.*)
>
> (**VIOLETTA** *coughs, and* **CHRIS** *glances over at her.*)
>
> (*Beat.*)

CHRIS. What's that mean?

BILLY. What?

CHRIS. (*Butchering the accent.*) "Kien essel mama wavos"?

BILLY. "Huevos."

CHRIS. Yeah.

BILLY. "Eggs," you know.

CHRIS. Like huevos rancheros?

BILLY. Yeah. Like huevos rancheros.

CHRIS. Why's he talking about eggs?

BILLY. (*Gesturing.*) EGGS.

CHRIS. Oh. I get it.

BILLY. Christ. Your español is really for shit these days, huh? Shoulda started bringing you down there with me, years ago…

> (**VIOLETTA** *coughs again.*)
>
> (**CHRIS** *glances over at her.*)
>
> (*She looks at the floor.*)
>
> (*Blackout.*)

Scene Two

(The dimly-lit, filthy hallway of a tenement building in Phoenix. **NINI**, *twenty-six, pounds on an apartment door.)*

(There is no answer. He knocks again, louder.)

(A baby inside the apartment starts to scream.)

NINI. Hello? Hey, hello?

(He pounds on the door.)

¿Abuela? It's me. Answer the door!

(There is the sound of footsteps padding down a hallway inside the apartment, and then a **TIRED WOMAN***'s voice.)*

TIRED WOMAN. *(Offstage.)* Yes? ¿Sí?

NINI. Abuela. Abre la puerta.

TIRED WOMAN. *(Offstage.)* ¿Quién es?

NINI. Ninito – abre!

TIRED WOMAN. *(Offstage.)* Who you looking for?

NINI. Ay, lo siento... Rosa Marrón?

TIRED WOMAN. *(Offstage.)* No here.

NINI. Oh... You know when she come home?

TIRED WOMAN. *(Offstage.)* What time is it?

NINI. Sorry. Es muy tarde.

TIRED WOMAN. *(Offstage.)* She don't live here no more, okay? She gone.

NINI. Gone? Where she go?

TIRED WOMAN. *(Offstage.)* Desaparecida.

NINI. She leave something for me? A letter, or...

(No answer. **NINI** *pounds on the door.)*

Excuse me? Hello? Hey – Por fa'...Come back. This her grandson, Nini. She told me, come to this address. She must have leaved something...

(The door opens a crack. It is chained from the inside.)

TIRED WOMAN. *(Offstage.)* There's nothing, joven. Adios.

(She starts to shut the door, but NINI *jams his fingers in the crack to keep it from closing.)*

NINI. Wait. Please –

TIRED WOMAN. *(Offstage.)* ¿Qué haces? Suéltala –

NINI. Please, she would have leaved something – I need it!

TIRED WOMAN. *(Offstage.) (Shouting.)* Carlos – Hey, Carlos! Help – ¡Hay un loco en la puerta! Carlos!

*(*NINI *steps back and she slams the door, bolts it.)*

*(*NINI *stands there, panting, listening to the baby scream. He rests his forehead against the metal door.)*

Scene Three

(The truck dispatch office. Later. A patter of rain on the plastic sheets.)

(VIOLETTA is still in the chair.)

(BILLY and CHRIS sit on the couch now, drinking beers, nudging pots and Tupperware containers around with their feet to catch the leaks.)

BILLY. …Went to see your mother, on my way back.

CHRIS. Oh yeah?

BILLY. You oughta, y'know – At some point.

CHRIS. I will.

BILLY. Soon. She'd like a visit. Surprise her. Will you?

CHRIS. All right.

BILLY. She's dropped some weight, you know. Ten, twenty pounds. New system they got there. Fruit diet.

CHRIS. Food's probably for shit.

BILLY. Looks good on her though. You should see. A different person.

CHRIS. Yeah.

BILLY. She could always stand to lose a few. But she's got a great figure.

CHRIS. I don't want to talk about her figure, Pop, all right? If you don't mind?

BILLY. No.

(CHRIS shoots his empty at the trash can like it's a basketball hoop. He probably misses.)

CHRIS. So what's she doing now?

BILLY. You know, Bingo, Checkers… What have you.

CHRIS. They got Bingo there?

BILLY. Oh yeah. Lawn bowling. Swimming pool. Didn't see it all myself, but apparently –

CHRIS. So she's all right then.

BILLY. Seems fine, I guess. Doesn't much like being there… Cried when I left, y'know. Wanted to come home today. Says she feels much better. Don't know why they're keeping her. But as I'm leaving, she makes a move for my belt, so –

> (**CHRIS** *makes a noise.*)

Anyways, she sends her love.

CHRIS. Humping your leg, right?

BILLY. What?

CHRIS. "Move for your belt –" Ha.

BILLY. It's an illness. That's your mother you're talking about –

> (*Suddenly,* **VIOLETTA***, who has been looking increasingly ill, throws up against the wall.*)

CHRIS. Jesus!

> (*They watch her gag, dry-heave.*)

What's wrong with her?

BILLY. Probably the truck.

CHRIS. Uh. Stinks.

> (*Beat.*)

I'm not cleaning it up, either, Pop. If that's what you think. You brought her here. You do it.

> (*To* **VIOLETTA**.)

Hey – You sick? What do you have? Hey – Sick or what? Uh…

BILLY. Enfermo.

CHRIS. Enfermo?

> (*She nods. They both look at her.*)

We should check if she's got a temperature.

BILLY. What are you, a fucking doctor now?

CHRIS. She could be really sick. I don't know. Maybe she needs some medicine, or –

BILLY. Well, you be my guest…

(**CHRIS** *approaches* **VIOLETTA**. *He reaches out a hand to touch her.*)

(*She shrinks away.*)

CHRIS. Trying to help –

(*A knock at the door.*)

BILLY. Finally… Go get that piece of shit.

(*Another knock.*)

(**CHRIS** *crosses the room and opens the door.*)

(**NINI** *enters, carrying a soggy bag of fast food and a package wrapped in shiny red foil.*)

(*He goes straight to* **VIOLETTA** *with the bag, takes out a burger, unwraps it, and offers it to her. She pushes it away.*)

(*He sees the vomit on the wall.*)

NINI. Mierda… ¿Estás bien?

VIOLETTA. No aguantaba más.

NINI. ¿Tienes hambre? ¿Puedes comer algo?

(*She nods.* **NINI** *unwraps the package, takes out a little souvenir snow globe. He shows it to her.*)

"Phoenix," eh?

BILLY. You got something for me, too?

(**NINI** *squeezes* **VIOLETTA**'s *hand. He gives her the globe.*)

NINI. Hey, Billy – Listen, amigo. There was a little mixed-up. Um…

BILLY. You're late.

NINI. I know. Just temporary, see…

(*Forces a laugh.*)

I couldn't get the rest of the fees yet, man. Bad communications, you know? Nobody home.

(*Beat.*)

You know what I think happen, Billy? Mi abuela probably come looking for me, to give the money. But she don't know where to go, right? She a old lady. You know how they be. She probably, right now, by the station. Looking at all the people coming out, like – "¿Señor, usted ha visto mi nieto, Nini?" And thinks I'm gonna come off the bus with a suitcase and flowers. Fresh from Mexico, you know? Probably waiting on her flowers...

BILLY. What's that got to do with me?

NINI. Tomorrow, Billy, I find her. Go to her workplace. It's all right. Just bad luck, tonight, is all.

BILLY. Maybe they already got her. You think of that? La Migra? Maybe she's gone.

NINI. No no no, I talk to her, two days past, Billy. She's here. I swear.

BILLY. *(Shoots* **CHRIS** *a look.)* What about your friends? Your homeboys? You've done favors for people, haven't you?

NINI. Yeah sure, but they don't have this kind of – plata though.

BILLY. No?

NINI. Not my friends.

BILLY. You'd be surprised... What people have. Stashed away someplace.

NINI. I already ask, Billy. Before I leave. I ask every person I know, just to get half we pay.

BILLY. That's not my problem though, is it?

NINI. No. You right. Tomorrow, Billy. I swear...

> *(Beat.)*

BILLY. I got another run to do. Tonight.

NINI. Sí.

BILLY. Picking up some people down Nuevo Laredo way. Be back in a day or two. Once I drop 'em off.

NINI. Yes, okay...

BILLY. And the girl stays here, with Chris. Collateral. You know what that means?

(**NINI** *shakes his head.*)

(**CHRIS** *glances at* **VIOLETTA**. *She's looking down at the floor.*)

BILLY. It means you bring the money back, amigo, or we're keeping her. ¿Comprende? Is that clear enough for you?

NINI. Sí. I understand this. Thank you very much, Bill.

BILLY. Call your friends, Ninito. Call your fucking primos. Tell them – your mother's dying. Tell them she got the cancer. Tell them the truth: you don't come up with a thousand dollars by Monday morning, an American coyote's gonna sell your lady friend to the whorehouse behind the taquería. You tell them that. Whole village'll be lined up at Western Union by morning, wiring pesos, right? You'll be the Mexican George Bailey, kid. You don't know how loved you really are!

Scene Four

(Later.)

*(**BILLY** and **NINI** are gone.)*

*(**VIOLETTA** sits in the same position as before.)*

*(**CHRIS** is at the desk, pretending to read the paper, but sneaking furtive glances at her around the headlines.)*

(A foot-long sledgehammer sits on the desk next to him, within easy reach.)

VIOLETTA. Perdón, Señor –

CHRIS. Hm?

VIOLETTA. Disculpa –

CHRIS. What's that?

VIOLETTA. Disculpa, Señor…¿necesito usar el baño?

(Beat.)

CHRIS. I – Uh… No español. Sorry.

VIOLETTA. ¿Baño? Necesito usar el –

CHRIS. Wanted to learn, you know? In high school? Dropped out. No español on the GED.

(He laughs.)

So… I can just say like – buenos días. That's about it. "Buenos días, Señorita."

VIOLETTA. Buenas tardes.

CHRIS. Whatever.

(Beat.)

Hey – You're fucking beautiful, know that?

VIOLETTA. Necesito usar el baño… Es urgente, por fa'?

CHRIS. Maybe your boyfriend can translate. When he comes back, you know? *If* he comes back… We could talk. Like with the subtitles –

(Gibberish.)

Onda locka chicka poco toco myoko.

(Pretending to read words in the air.)

CHRIS. I'm a hot Mexican chick and I think you're super-cool.

VIOLETTA. *(Frustrated.)* Señor?

CHRIS. Hey – *Is* he your boyfriend? Cousin? You two related or what?

(Laughs.)

Probably not, right? I ain't that lucky. Gotta catch the good ones between guys, or you got no shot…

VIOLETTA. Please, the bathroom? Okay?

(Beat.)

(**CHRIS** *looks at her.*)

CHRIS. Bathroom?

VIOLETTA. Sí. Baño?

CHRIS. Wait – You speak English?

VIOLETTA. ¿Baño? Por favor, ¿Señor? Por fa–

CHRIS. No, come on. Don't. Don't do that. Don't go back to – Am I hearing things? Didn't you just say "bathroom?"

VIOLETTA. No hablo – Necesito usar el baño.

CHRIS. You speak. Am I crazy? I heard you. Hey – We could talk. Have a conversation. We could speak some, if you understand…

(Long pause.)

VIOLETTA. Sí. A little bit. Okay.

CHRIS. Holy shit! "A little bit." Why didn't you say so? I'm talking to myself like a fucking asshole over here, and you're all –

VIOLETTA. No, you are not –

CHRIS. What?

VIOLETTA. Not a –

CHRIS. What, "asshole"?

VIOLETTA. Ah.

CHRIS. You know that word?

(*Beat.*)

VIOLETTA. Sí.

CHRIS. Oh my God! You're like, completely fluent, and I'm up here like –

VIOLETTA. No no, just a little. I don't –

CHRIS. Hey – What's your name? Tell me that? At least. Tu namo es…?

VIOLETTA. Violetta.

CHRIS. Violetta. That's nice. Damn. That's a really nice name, you know?

VIOLETTA. Gracias.

CHRIS. No, speak English, come on. Just say "thank you" like a normal person, okay? I'm Chris, right? Chris? Can you say that?

VIOLETTA. Chris.

CHRIS. Good to meet you, Violetta.

VIOLETTA. Good to meet you also.

CHRIS. So, tell me like – where you're from, and – What kind of shit you like to do. I mean… Damn! What a relief finally to meet somebody who can communicate a little –

VIOLETTA. I can no. Sorry.

CHRIS. Can no? How come?

VIOLETTA. No allowed.

CHRIS. What? Who says?

(*Beat.*)

VIOLETTA. Nini. Tell me you are danger to me. "No hables con los coyotes. Te abusan. Tal vez te violan."

CHRIS. Me? I am?

(*He laughs.*)

Come on. Do I look dangerous to you?

VIOLETTA. (*Correcting herself.*) "Danger*ous*," sí…

CHRIS. Come on. You want some coffee? Uh… "cafe"?

(He gets up and takes a thermos from the desk.)

CHRIS. I'm gonna have some. We can talk. You want some? Have some, all right?

VIOLETTA. Thank you.

CHRIS. You're welc– Uh, de nada.

VIOLETTA. Ah.

CHRIS. What?

VIOLETTA. ¿Hablas español?

CHRIS. Come on. You making fun of me?

VIOLETTA. No. "De nada" you say…

CHRIS. Yeah, I'm like – half retarded. Pick up a few words at the taco stand. Don't even know the word for "bathroom." And you're all "Yes, monsieur, indeed I am familiar with the term asshole."

VIOLETTA. Hey – In Tijuana? This is very important word.

(Beat.)

(He laughs.)

CHRIS. Yeah… I can see that… I get it. Hey, you got a good sense of humor, you know that? How'd you learn to talk English? Most Mexicans I meet, they just look at you like –

(He imitates them.)

– Juan Valdez, dumbshit farmers, you know? Don't speak. Don't blink. Just stare –

VIOLETTA. I grow up on border. Everybody they speak a little.

CHRIS. Oh, no shit, yeah. TJ. What do you do there?

VIOLETTA. Me? I work.

CHRIS. Doing what?

VIOLETTA. At a club.

CHRIS. Cool. Like a waitress or something?

(He gives her the coffee.)

There you go.

VIOLETTA. Thank you.

CHRIS. De nada…

(He laughs, sits down.)

CHRIS. So damn – It's good to have somebody to talk to! You know, Pop's always taking these trips down over the line. Leaves me here, gotta sit with the mojados in transit. No TV. No PlayStation. Stare at the wall all day. Start to go mentally ill in Amityville, know what I mean? I'm just so relieved you're actually like –

VIOLETTA. Hey – Mister Chris?

CHRIS. Hm?

VIOLETTA. …Sorry, I interrupt?

CHRIS. No, no, it's okay. I want you to talk. I like it. What?

VIOLETTA. Um… Okay I use bathroom now, or –

*(**CHRIS** jumps out of his chair, embarrassed.)*

CHRIS. Yeah yeah, sorry… I completely forget. I forgot. So excited, just… Right through there – Here. Through that door.

(She nods.)

You gotta jiggle the flush a little bit.

(He demonstrates.)

Jiggle? Y'know?

VIOLETTA. Okay. Gracias.

(She goes in the bathroom, starts to shut the door.)

CHRIS. Hey, Violetta –

VIOLETTA. ¿Sí?

CHRIS. Not "Mister," okay? Just Chris.

VIOLETTA. Just Chris.

CHRIS. A'ight?

(She nods, goes into the bathroom, and shuts the door.)

(**CHRIS** *pushes the chairs together, arranging a little sitting area. He tries to tidy the desk, gathers the empty beer cans and tosses them in the trash.*)

(*He cups his hands over his mouth and smells his breath.*)

(*Not good enough.*)

(*He rummages in the desk and finds a bottle of blue Listerine.*)

(*He takes a swig, swishes it around in his mouth, looks for a place to spit.*)

(*The sound of the flush from the bathroom.*)

(**VIOLETTA** *enters.*)

(**CHRIS** *swallows the Listerine.*)

VIOLETTA. Gracias.

CHRIS. Uch.

VIOLETTA. Okay?

CHRIS. (*Hoarse.*) Fine, yeah. How you doing?

VIOLETTA. Me, I no feel so good.

CHRIS. No? Why?

VIOLETTA. Throw up again.

CHRIS. Now?

VIOLETTA. No, in – You don't hear?

CHRIS. No, I was – I wasn't listening. You want some mouthwash?

VIOLETTA. No. Thank you.

　　　　(*He puts the Listerine away.*)

Sorry…

CHRIS. No, it's –

VIOLETTA. I try to clean.

CHRIS. It's all right. Hey. Don't worry. Okay? I'll take care of it. We've had worse, believe me. In there. How you feel now? Better?

VIOLETTA. Little dizzy.

CHRIS. Can I –

> *(Feels her forehead.)*

Shit, you're burning.

VIOLETTA. I am scared…

CHRIS. You're okay.

VIOLETTA. You call doctor? If I need?

CHRIS. You won't need. Why?

> *(She starts to cry. He looks at her.)*

What? You're okay. Little fever's all. What do you need? Hey – I'll get you something, all right? Make you feel better. Some medicine?

VIOLETTA. Medicina?

CHRIS. Sí. What kind?

VIOLETTA. I don't know in English…

CHRIS. No problem. Write it down.

> *(He gives her a pad of paper.)*

Write in Spanish. Walmart down the road'll figure it out. Used to dealing with you uh –

VIOLETTA. Okay.

> *(She scribbles something on the pad.)*

CHRIS. Yeah?

VIOLETTA. Sí. Gracias…

CHRIS. No doubt. Uh. I'm gonna have to tie you up though, all right? While I'm gone.

> *(Beat.)*

VIOLETTA. What?

CHRIS. I have to tie you. To the chair, you know –

> *(He mimes tying her.)*

VIOLETTA. I am sick.

CHRIS. Yeah, but… You know, if you leave while I'm gone, my pop would murder me.

VIOLETTA. I will no leave.

CHRIS. I know, but – Come on. That's a thousand bucks, Violetta, right? I can't just –

VIOLETTA. You no have to tie me, Chris. Don't have to do this. I stay. Wait here for you.

CHRIS. Yeah, but how do you expect me to – I mean, I trust you and all, but –

VIOLETTA. ¿Sí?

CHRIS. I can't. All right? I'm sorry, but – We just met. And I can't.

VIOLETTA. You tie me? Like a cow?

CHRIS. I mean – Come on.

VIOLETTA. It hurt my hands.

CHRIS. Look – Just a couple minutes, all right? I'll be right back. Ten minutes, okay?

VIOLETTA. What if I am sick again? What if I pee?

CHRIS. You serious?

VIOLETTA. Yes I am serious. What? Just sit here and – on myself?

> (*He shrugs helplessly.*)
>
> (*Beat.*)
>
> (*She sits down in the chair, offers her hands.*)
>
> (*He starts to tie her hands with a length of electrical cord.*)

CHRIS. I'm sorry... Y'know? I wish I could help more. I want to be nice to you and everything. You seem like a really nice person to me, but...

> (*He finishes tying her hands.*)

VIOLETTA. Ay.

CHRIS. That hurt? Sorry. Shit.

> (*Pause.*)

Don't go nowhere, all right? I'll be right back.

(He exits.)

(The sound of a car starting, with difficulty.)

*(**VIOLETTA** pulls at the cord, trying to free her hands. No luck. She sighs.)*

Scene Five

(A public phone in Phoenix.)

(NINI *drops in some quarters, dials, waits.)*

NINI. Hey carnal, it's Nini, man. ¿Qué onda? Tranquilo, I'm – How you doing?

(Pause.)

Listen, guey, I need to ask you something. All right? Big favor. But don't be pissed off at me or nothing, all right?

(Pause.)

I know, but – I need your help, 'mano. It's important. Sumamente. You know what I'm saying? I need help, just for –

(Pause.)

Twelve hundred.

(Pause.)

I know, 'mano! But you – Listen, you got your Volkswagen, right? You got that. Have to be worth at least like –

(Pause.)

I would pay you back, man! I pay. I buy you new car. Same kind. Be making ends now. In the States, like you. Just one thousand, okay? With interest.

(Pause.)

Carnal, listen – It's because my mama – She have the cáncer, guey…

(He pretends to cry.)

She have to go to the hospital and she – She ain't got no money, man. She need quimio and shit, and –

(Pause.)

Yeah, so I thought – You and me, right? My best friend in the whole fucking world, man, you know that. No, *you* are. I look up to you, and – Like a older brother to me…

(*Pause.*)

NINI. I know you love that car, man. I know you do. Guey, I'm asking you, please… For me… Compadres, eh…?

(*Pause.*)

Well fuck you then, ¡hijo de puta! My mama dying, you won't even sell your rusty piece-of-shit Jetta? For my mama, guey? I can't believe you!

(*Pause.*)

I hope you die, 'mano… Hope you get in crash and rip your face open and stick that VW steering wheel up your *ass*, man! You like it so much – Fucking maricón!

(*He slams the phone down.*)

(*Beat.*)

(*He starts to cry for real.*)

Scene Six

(The safe house. VIOLETTA is tied to the chair.)

(CHRIS enters, carrying an armload of clothes and sundries. He sets them down on the desk.)

CHRIS. Violetta? I got it. They didn't ask to see no prescription or nothing…

(He unties her, avoiding her eyes. She rubs her wrists.)

Hey – you hungry? I could make us eggs. You like eggs? Uh… Huevos?

(VIOLETTA shakes her head.)

CHRIS. What do you want then? Cheese sandwich? Uh… Queso de…sandwich?

VIOLETTA. No.

CHRIS. I'm sorry, all right? It's not up to me. My dad could go to jail. Don't be mad.

VIOLETTA. I can no feel my hands.

(Beat.)

CHRIS. I brought you some things. Look. Shampoo and clothes. From my ma's closet. She got a hundred pounds on you, probably, but –

(He sorts through the clothes.)

Got some…jeans. Sweatshirt. Socks and…you know –

(Embarrassed, he quickly folds the underwear.)

I don't know if you want to change, but – I thought if you have to stay here a while… You know, might want to take a shower, or – Clean up a bit. Got you a razor, too. "Venus Divine." Huh? The one in the bathroom's like a butter knife. Two hundred Mexicans shaved their crossing beards with that rusty piece of shit. Cut you up ruthless if you try to do your legs, or…

(Pushes the pile toward her.)

CHRIS. For you. It's all for you. Understand?

    *(***VIOLETTA** *nods.)*

I think there's hot water now. In case you want to take a bath. It's fucking cold, right? Like a refrigerator. The desert. People think it's hot, because there's no rain or snow, but... Come on. You're not hungry? What do you want? Try to eat something. You'll feel better. Probably been like, days since you – I have um – M&M's. You want some? Chocolata? Have some, all right? We'll both have some.

    (Beat.)

VIOLETTA. Okay.

CHRIS. Good. Okay.

    (He gives her some M&M's. She eats. He watches her.)

Jesus, I was right, huh? You're starved.

VIOLETTA. *(Mouth full.)* Lo siento... Sorry. Have no manner.

CHRIS. No, it's fine. I'm glad. I'll get some more. Next time. They're like fifty cents at the Circle K. If I'da known you like 'em. Woulda got more. Check it: we got a hot plate too. I could make us some real food.

    (Unloads the supplies on the desk.)

Got uh – Rice-A-Ronis. You like that?

VIOLETTA. "Ronis"? I don't know.

CHRIS. "Mexican-style." You'll like it, I bet. You want to try?

VIOLETTA. Okay.

CHRIS. Okay then.

    (He opens the box, plugs in the hot plate.)

Must be tired, after that ride.

VIOLETTA. Sí...

CHRIS. That's a rough trip, I know. Under those bananas... I been down there a couple times, helping Pop swab out the floor. Smell'll give you nightmares. We got a mattress. You could lie down in back, if you want. After dinner?

(VIOLETTA nods.)

You can relax now. It's all right. I'll be right here. Don't worry. Nothing's gonna happen to you while I'm around…

Scene Seven

(The safe house. Night. **CHRIS** *sits at the desk, rolling a joint.)*

(From outside, we hear **NINI** *singing.* **CHRIS** *looks up.)*

NINI. *(Offstage.)*
TENGO MI PAR DE PISTOLAS
CON SUS CACHAS DE MARFIL,
PARA DARME DE BALAZOS
CON LOS DEL FERROCARRIL...

*(***CHRIS** *puts his hand on the hammer.)*

(The front door slams open and **NINI** *staggers in, carrying an open tequila bottle wrapped in a brown paper bag, and another package of fast food.)*

(He sings drunkenly.)

TENGO MI PAR DE PISTOLAS
CON SU PARQUE MUY CABAL,
UNA PARA MI QUERIDA
Y OTRA PARA MI RIVAL...

CHRIS. Shh!

NINI. *(Sings a Mexican howl.)*
AYYYYAAYAYAYA!

CHRIS. Yo – Shut the fuck up, man!

*(***NINI** *looks at him blearily.)*

NINI. What?

CHRIS. Violetta's sleeping... You'll wake her up, man!

NINI. She sleep?

CHRIS. Yeah. That's what I been telling you. In the back.

NINI. Where?

CHRIS. We got a AeroBed.

*(***NINI** *goes past him and glances into the other room. He comes back out.)*

NINI. She eat dinner?

CHRIS. I made Rice-A-Ronis, yeah.

(**NINI** *looks at him.*)

NINI. Ronis?

CHRIS. She liked it, man. Ate a whole package and everything. Don't worry.

(**NINI** *sits heavily down on the floor, takes a swig of liquor, and leans his head against the wall, exhausted.*)

NINI. Okay… Gracias.

CHRIS. De nada.

(**NINI** *snorts at his pronunciation.*)

What?

NINI. Nothing.

(**CHRIS** *looks him over. He lets go of the hammer.*)

CHRIS. Didn't get it, huh?

NINI. What?

CHRIS. The money, man. Didn't find your granny?

NINI. No. She gone. Desaparacida…

(*He makes a gesture – "Poof!" Laughs drunkenly.*)

CHRIS. So what you been doing all day? You been gone like – twelve hours or something.

NINI. Me? I stand on corner, you know. People go by, I say, "Please, Mister, spare the change? My mama sick." They walk around, try not to look at me, like –

(*He imitates a guy trying to avoid eye contact.*)

CHRIS. So how much you get?

NINI. Enough for chicken. And tequila…

(*He laughs, takes a swig.*)

CHRIS. That's fucked up, man… Got that girl counting on you back there. Watching the door all day, waiting. And you're out getting plowed…

NINI. Money don't grow on trees, hermano. Even here.

(CHRIS finishes rolling the joint, licks it closed, and takes out a lighter.)

(He glances at NINI. NINI's eyes are almost closed.)

CHRIS. Hey – You smoke?

NINI. What?

CHRIS. Smoke, man. Smoke pot? Smoke weed? You don't do that in Mexico?

NINI. No man, we say NO to that where I come from…

CHRIS. For real?

> *(Beat.)*

Oh, you're joking. You're joking, right? I get it. Here –

> *(He holds out the joint. NINI pinches it in his fingers, takes a drag.)*

Don't tell my pop though, all right? He don't like it while I'm working.

NINI. Sí. Violetta don't like it while I working neither…

> *(CHRIS laughs.)*

CHRIS. Bet.

> *(NINI holds out his bottle.)*

NINI. You want?

CHRIS. No, man.

NINI. Come on. You give me smoke, I pay you back. Like NAFTA.

> *(He holds out the bottle.)*

> *(CHRIS takes a little sip.)*

¡Maricón! Like this –

> *(He takes the bottle back and takes a long swig, chokes, laughs.)*

> *(He holds out the bottle, and CHRIS takes another sip. He puckers his lips.)*

CHRIS. Damn, that's some cheap shit, man…

NINI. ¡Calidad!

CHRIS. Fucking Mexican bootleg rubbing alcohol.

NINI. We invented this, man! Your shit is bootleg. This is original Sauza Blanco!

CHRIS. All right, man, whatever.

NINI. With your fucked up U.S. verde… What you talking about, "bootleg"?

>*(CHRIS laughs.)*

>*(They sit quietly for a while, smoking and drinking, relaxed.)*

CHRIS. Hey – What the hell does that mean, anyway? "Nini"?

NINI. Nothing. Don't mean nothing.

CHRIS. In Spanish? Your name don't mean nothing?

NINI. No. You?

CHRIS. Chris? Yeah.

NINI. What?

CHRIS. Jesus, man.

NINI. Oh, sí. Jesus. That's nice…

CHRIS. So why they call you Nini then? It's short for something?

NINI. Yeah. Negro.

CHRIS. Nay-ghro?

NINI. Sí.

CHRIS. How you spell that?

NINI. N-E-G-R-O.

>*(CHRIS snorts.)*

What?

CHRIS. Nothing, man – Forget it.

NINI. Why you do that?

CHRIS. You serious? Your name is Negro?

NINI. Negro. American word, no?

CHRIS. Yeah. Yeah, I know what it means in American. I just don't know if it means what you think it means.

NINI. Black person.

CHRIS. Yeah.

NINI. Sí.

(*Beat.*)

CHRIS. Okay, fine… That's your name.

NINI. Sí. When I am born, I have the extreme dark skin, dark eyes, you know? A black baby. Everybody has this kind of baby name in Mexico. Black baby, white baby. My cousin "Blanca"? Is very common.

CHRIS. Not here.

NINI. In my town.

CHRIS. All right. Negro then. That's your name. I wouldn't, you know… Probably shouldn't introduce yourself – Like, go around to parties, "Yo wassup, it's motherfucking Negro in the house!"

(**NINI** *laughs, takes another hit.*)

NINI. I won't do that, no.

CHRIS. Hey – You feel it yet?

NINI. Sí… It's good…

CHRIS. Ha. Told you, motherfucker. Chronic.

NINI. Calidad…

CHRIS. Sí.

(*They pass the joint back and forth.*)

NINI. Hey, I got a joke for you in Spanish, you want to know?

CHRIS. I don't speak Spanish.

NINI. I know you don't speak. You understand. It's easy joke.

CHRIS. I'm not gonna understand any Spanish though. Believe me. Tell it in English.

NINI. Not funny in English. You want to hear or no?

CHRIS. Yeah… Okay, man, sí. Tell that shit.

NINI. Okay, so – It's in the forest, right? Gotta know this. In the forest. A mono – "monkey" and a – How you say "Iguana"?

CHRIS. Iguana. Iguana.

NINI. Iguana? That's how you say?

> *(Laughs.)*

Okay. That's fucked up. Bueno. Mono and Iguana. In the forest. Up in the tree, right? And mono –

> *(He demonstrates.)*

Smoking, okay?

> *(CHRIS laughs.)*

(Switching into Spanish.) Iguana viene, y dice al mono "Señor Mono, ¿qué estás haciendo?" Y el mono: "Fumando marijuana. Fumando marijuana."

CHRIS. What the fuck?

NINI. *(Demonstrating.)* Fumando marijuana. He say he smoking weed. And the iguana go, "Señor Mono, ¿puedo probar un poco de eso?" Iguana toma el churro y lo fuma. Y el mono: "¿Sientes eso?" Y el Iguana: "No siento nada."

CHRIS. What's that?

NINI. Iguana smoke some, but he don't feel nothing. He say "No siento nada." "I don't feel nothing."

CHRIS. Uh-huh. Okay.

NINI. Y el monkey: "Fuma más. Fuma más."

> *(CHRIS laughs.)*

So Igauna –

> *(He mimes smoking.)*

Fuma más, right? Mono: "¿Qué sientes ahora?" Iguana: "Yo no siento nada." Mono: "Fuma más. Fuma más." So. Finalmente, el churro se acaba, y el mono dice "Fumaste todo mi churro, Señor Iguana. ¿Todavía no sientes nada?" Y el iguana: "No... Yo no siento nada. No siento mis brazos... No siento mis piernas... No siento mi cara..."

CHRIS. Wait – Wait –

NINI. What?

CHRIS. That's the joke?

NINI. Sí. You don't get?

CHRIS. No, I get... I get it, yeah... That's fucking hilarious, yo!

NINI. See? Told you.

CHRIS. You looked just like that monkey!

NINI. Fuck you man. You look like the monkey.

CHRIS. No, you really – I mean you did that shit so well! "Fumandez marijuana... Fumandez mas..." Fucking stoner monkey...

(He imitates **NINI** *smoking like a monkey.)*

NINI. Don't tell me I look like monkey, puto.

CHRIS. Why not?

NINI. Because. It's racist.

CHRIS. What? I'm saying YOU look like a monkey, man. Not everybody – I'm not generalizing. Not every Mexican in the world looks like a monkey or something. Just fucking Negro –

NINI. Negro.

CHRIS. Nay-ghro, whatever.

NINI. White people always saying other people look like monkey, man. That's why it's racist.

CHRIS. Fuck that –

NINI. That's true.

CHRIS. I ain't white. So.

*(***NINI*** makes a sound of disbelief.)*

I'm a quarter Papago Indian, bitch. My pop's on the tribal council. What now?

NINI. Indian?

CHRIS. Yeah.

> (**NINI** *looks him over.*)

NINI. From where?

CHRIS. From here, Arizona! Papago.

NINI. Where your feathers at?

CHRIS. I don't wear feathers, man. That's a stereotype.

NINI. Then you're white to me, okay? Gringo? Ain't got no feathers, you white.

CHRIS. Oh yeah? So where's your – whatever-the-fuck you people – Where's your sombrero, man?

> (**NINI** *laughs.*)

You think I'm racist? For real?

NINI. Hell yeah.

CHRIS. No, really. You think I am?

NINI. Yes. Really.

CHRIS. Man, fuck you. You don't know me.

NINI. Fuck you also.

CHRIS. Can't believe you're calling me racist. Name is fucking Negro, calling me a racist. Okay.

NINI. (*Pronouncing it.*) Negro.

CHRIS. Nay-ghro, negro. Whatever. Your father was racist. Fucking Mexicans are racist.

NINI. At least he not malora. Eh?

> (*Beat.*)

CHRIS. Don't say that, okay?

NINI. Say what?

CHRIS. Say – whatever it is you just said about him, man. Don't say that.

NINI. You don't know what I said.

CHRIS. I know it wasn't good.

NINI. Maybe I say he Uncle Sam. Jorge Washington, eh?

CHRIS. You don't know him, all right?

NINI. I know he is coyote. Traficante de seres humanos.

CHRIS. He has stomach problems.

NINI. What the fuck?!

CHRIS. Cross-country hauls shake up your belly, man. You don't know that? You ever move a rig thirty, forty-five hours in a stretch? No break? No sleep? Peeing in a Dixie cup? Squeezing your ass the whole way because you can't make time to go to the can even once? Have to eat bananas and Imodium A-D just to make it through that shift. Shit blood by the time you're through... Over the border's like two hours. Make as much in a day as you make in a week doing the long haul. He don't want to do this, man. Don't have no choice.

NINI. I don't care, man. What the fuck that has to do with me? Drink some Pepto-Bismol. Wear some Pamper.

CHRIS. He's doing you a favor.

NINI. Favor? Bullshit. I pay.

CHRIS. Half.

NINI. I pay. No favor.

CHRIS. Nobody asked you to come...

NINI. You think I want to come here? That what you think? To this shithole? This Violetta's idea. Okay? Because she want her baby born here. American. Not to do with me. Nothing to do with me...

CHRIS. She's pregnant?

(*Beat.*)

NINI. Forget that, man, okay? Not to do with you either. Don't worry

CHRIS. You brought it up.

NINI. Anyway, I proud to be Mexican. Never want to come here. Love my town.

CHRIS. (*Laughs.*) Yeah, whatever, man.

NINI. What? What, whatever?

CHRIS. Everybody spouts that shit. Proud to be Mexican, proud to be Chinese, Korean, Mogadishuan, and everybody still hopping under a crate of drippy bananas to get here.

NINI. No, man…

CHRIS. Yes. Sí. People always talk about America, "Fuck America, fuck George Bush, fuck McDonalds." So why all you all still want to come?

NINI. Because! You rich imperialistas, man. Got all our money. That's why.

CHRIS. Because this is the greatest country in the world, amigo, and you motherfuckers know it.

NINI. Chinga tu madre, cabrón.

CHRIS. Chinga tu huevos.

> (*Beat.*)

NINI. (*Laughs.*) What? Where you learn that, man? Who taught you that stupid shit?

CHRIS. Don't worry about it… I got a GED. I ain't stupid.

> (*They sit there, drinking and smoking. Not speaking.*)

> (*After a while,* NINI *laughs.*)

NINI. Hey – You want to sing a song with me?

CHRIS. No.

NINI. Come on. You know a drunk song? For drinking?

CHRIS. Fuck you.

NINI. You don't know one of those?

CHRIS. Uh-uh, man. No. I don't.

NINI. You angry?

CHRIS. No…

NINI. So then. A drunken song. American drinking song about alcohol. You don't have these?

CHRIS. About alcohol? Yeah. We have I think –

NINI. Yeah.

CHRIS. I think so.

NINI. All right. Teach me. I like to learn.

> (*Pause.*)

CHRIS. All right, give me another sip though.

> *(He swigs from the bottle, coughs.)*

> *(They both laugh.)*

CHRIS. My ma used to sing this to me when she came home. All bombed… Late at night. Get in bed smelling like the boys at the chop shop. Titties all hanging out…

NINI. Your mama, guey?

CHRIS. Yeah.

NINI. Damn, fuck that…

CHRIS. Okay, you ready?

NINI. Sí. I ready. Go.

CHRIS. I don't have a good voice though… But check it –
NINETY-NINE BOTTLES OF BEER ON THE WALL. NINETY–NINE BOTTLES OF BEER. TAKE ONE DOWN, PASS IT AROUND, NINETY-EIGHT BOTTLES OF BEER ON THE WALL… NINETY–EIGHT BOTTLES OF BEER ON THE WALL, NINETY-EIGHT BOTTLES OF BEER. TAKE ONE DOWN, PASS IT AROUND, NINETY-SEVEN BOTTLES OF BEER ON THE WALL. NINETY-SEVEN BOTTLES OF BEER ON THE WALL –

NINI. Wait wait wait.

CHRIS. What?

NINI. That's the whole thing? Like that?

CHRIS. Yeah.

NINI. Just keep going?

CHRIS. Keep going and going.

NINI. *(Laughs.)* Okay. I see.

CHRIS. Okay then. You ready?

NINI. Why on the wall though?

CHRIS. I don't know.

NINI. All right. I ready then. How many?

CHRIS. Ninety-six.

NINI. Ninety-six. Okay

> *(Takes a drink, sings loudly.)*

NINETY-SIX BOTTLE OF BEER ON THE WALL!

NINETY-SIX BOTTLE OF BEER!

CHRIS.

TAKE ONE DOWN –

NINI.

WE PASS HIM AROUND.

CHRIS.

NINETY-FIVE BOTTLES OF BEER ON THE WALL!

CHRIS & NINI.

NINETY-FIVE BOTTLES OF BEER ON THE WALL!
NINETY-FIVE BOTTLES OF BEER!
TAKE ONE DOWN, PASS HIM AROUND!

CHRIS.

NINETY-FOUR BOTTLES OF –

*(In the middle of the line, **NINI** grabs the neck of the empty tequila bottle in one hand and smashes it across **CHRIS**' face.)*

*(The bottle shatters and **CHRIS** goes down, clutching his nose with both hands.)*

*(**NINI** stands over him, holding the bottle as if to stab him if he rises, but **CHRIS** stays on the floor.)*

*(**NINI** sweeps the sledgehammer off the desk into the corner of the room.)*

NINI. *(Shouting into the other room.)* ¡Ey! ¡Violetta! ¡Despiértate, nena! Arregla tus cosas – Apúrate, ¡no jodas!

*(He grabs the electrical cord from the floor, and with quick, sober movements, props **CHRIS** in the chair and kneels behind him, tying his hands.)*

*(**VIOLETTA** pokes her head into the room, wearing a long t-shirt, groggy with sleep.)*

(She sees them, freezes.)

VIOLETTA. ¿Ninito? ¿Qué haces?

NINI. ¡PONTE LA ROPA, MUCHACHA! ¡NOS VAMOS EN CHINGA!

(She runs back into the other room.)

(We can hear her frantically packing offstage, as **NINI** *fumbles with the knots.)*

CHRIS. Hey –

(Pause.)

Nini?

NINI. What?

CHRIS. I'm bleeding, man…

NINI. You're okay.

CHRIS. I'm fucking bleeding.

NINI. No es nada…

CHRIS. You broke my nose…

NINI. Tilt your head.

*(***CHRIS** *tilts his head back. He makes small gulping noises.)*

CHRIS. I'm swallowing blood, man… Think I'm gonna throw up.

NINI. No eres un chillón, man. You can't take care of your own fucking nosebleed?

CHRIS. *My* nosebleed?

NINI. Sí –

CHRIS. You hit me in the face with a tequila bottle, man! This is YOUR goddamn nosebleed!

*(***NINI** *finishes with the cord, stands up.)*

NINI. Sorry, okay?

CHRIS. You're sorry? Can't feel my cheeks…

(He tries to breathe, but can only manage a wet, rattling sound.)

Get me a tissue, man. Some Kleenex or –

NINI. Do I look like I got some Kleenex to you?

CHRIS. Toilet papers?

NINI. You run out.

CHRIS. Oh yeah.

(Rattling sound.)

CHRIS. I can't breathe. I'm choking...

> *(He tilts his head forward and blood splashes onto his chest.)*

(Hysterical.) SHIT!

NINI. What?

CHRIS. My shirt, man! Look –

NINI. Híjole, you scared me.

CHRIS. Scared you? I can't breathe!

> *(**NINI** gets up, goes behind the plastic sheeting.)*

> *(He returns with a roll of toilet paper, holds it out to **CHRIS**.)*

NINI. Here – Blow.

> *(**CHRIS** looks at him.)*

CHRIS. You been hiding it?

> *(Pause.)*

You stole my toilet paper, man? You know, this morning I had to wipe my ass with a FASHION MAGAZINE!

NINI. You want it or no?

> *(**NINI** holds the toilet paper to **CHRIS**' face, and **CHRIS** blows his nose.)*

> *(**NINI** tears off the tissue and throws it away.)*

CHRIS. I need to see a doctor.

NINI. You okay.

CHRIS. I think I might need stitches.

NINI. We not calling no doctor, all right? ¿Comprende? No happen.

> *(Calling into the back room.)*

Oye – ¿Qué chingados haces allí? ¿Apúrate, oíste?

> *(**VIOLETTA** enters from the back, wearing her dress from Scene One. She drags a heavy, battered suitcase behind her.)*

> *(**NINI** pushes a bandana into her hand.)*

NINI. Aquí – Asegúralo. Bien apretado. Ya vengo.

> (**NINI** *grabs the staple gun off the desk and sticks it in the back of his belt like a weapon. He takes the bag and exits through the front door.*)
>
> (**VIOLETTA** *looks at* **CHRIS.**)
>
> (*She spits in his face, and then wraps the bandana tightly around his head.*)
>
> (*The front door opens, and* **VIOLETTA** *speaks without turning around.*)

VIOLETTA. De todas maneras Ninito, ¿adónde vamos? No tenemos plata... No hay comida... Esto es loco, no joda –

> (**NINI** *enters, walking backwards, his eyes fixed on something outside.*)
>
> (*After a moment,* **BILLY** *comes through the door after him, holding a 12-gauge shotgun.*)
>
> (**VIOLETTA** *turns and sees him. She freezes.*)
>
> (**CHRIS** *mumbles something through his gag.*)

BILLY. (*Gesturing.*) Suéltalo.

> (**VIOLETTA** *quickly kneels behind* **CHRIS** *and unties his hands.*)
>
> (*He pulls the gag off his mouth.*)
>
> (*He coughs.*)

BILLY. You okay?

> (**CHRIS** *wipes his face with the bandana.*)

CHRIS. I wasn't looking, Pop. They snuck up on me.

BILLY. Didn't get the money, huh?

> (*Clucks his tongue.*)

All right, kid. You and me, going for a little ride. In the truck.

NINI. Billy – What about her, man?

BILLY. What about her? We never got paid, right? She stays.

> (*Blackout.*)

Scene Eight

(**BILLY** and **NINI** are gone.)

(**VIOLETTA** kneels in front of **CHRIS**, cleaning his face.)

(She holds a blood-stained towel and picks pieces of glass from his skin with tweezers, dropping them into a metal bowl on the floor.)

(He watches her guardedly, holding the hammer for protection.)

(They are both quiet for a long time.)

VIOLETTA. Lo siento, Christopher…

(**CHRIS** scoffs.)

I don't know words to say –

CHRIS. Don't then. I don't believe you anyways, so…

VIOLETTA. You are nice to me before. Tierno. Take care of me, when I am sick, and –

CHRIS. Just stop, all right? It's pathetic.

(She digs out another piece, drops it in the bowl.)

(He sucks his teeth.)

VIOLETTA. Sorry –

CHRIS. Hurry up. Don't talk.

VIOLETTA. I talk when I am scared.

(**VIOLETTA** pulls out another piece of glass.)

CHRIS. Ow!

VIOLETTA. Ay.

CHRIS. Careful, fuck! That stings! You trying to hurt me?

VIOLETTA. No, sorry. I be more careful now.

(He snatches the tweezers out of her hand.)

CHRIS. I'll do that shit.

(He glances into the bowl at his reflection and digs out a piece of glass, trying not to cry.)

CHRIS. Ah, man… Look at my face…

VIOLETTA. Chris…

CHRIS. It's broke, right?

VIOLETTA. What?

CHRIS. My nose? Is broken?

VIOLETTA. I think yes. Probably.

CHRIS. Shit… Gonna look all retarded now.

VIOLETTA. I don't know he will do that, Chris. I swear –

CHRIS. Whatever. Like you would've stopped it.

> (*He tries to breathe, snorts, blows a clot of blood out of his nose.*)

Fuck. Mojado broke my nose…

VIOLETTA. He scared.

> (**CHRIS** *scoffs.*)

Desesperado. He don't know what else to do…

> (*Beat.*)

Chris?

CHRIS. What?

VIOLETTA. What will happen now?

CHRIS. The fuck should I know?

VIOLETTA. Your father mandarlo al sur?

CHRIS. What?

VIOLETTA. Take Nini – down to Mexico?

CHRIS. I don't think so…

VIOLETTA. What then?

CHRIS. Probably take him out to the desert, most likely. Dig a hole.

> (*Beat.*)

VIOLETTA. Chris. I know you are angry…

CHRIS. No shit.

> (*He digs into his cheek, winces.*)
>
> (**VIOLETTA** *reaches for the tweezers.*)

(He hesitates, and then lets her take them.)

(She wipes some of the blood off his nose and goes back to work on his face.)

VIOLETTA. I ask you something?

CHRIS. What?

VIOLETTA. A favor.

CHRIS. HA!

VIOLETTA. I know I have no right. After what happen. I ask anyways. You call your father? Ask him let Nini go –

CHRIS. For what?

VIOLETTA. Please?

CHRIS. Why would I fucking do that? Huh? Even if he would listen to me, which he fucking wouldn't – That beanbag hurt me! Broke my nose!

VIOLETTA. I know –

CHRIS. When I was just trying to be friends! Talking English. Sharing my weed –

VIOLETTA. Sí. You are nice guy.

CHRIS. Ha.

VIOLETTA. You are.

CHRIS. You don't know me.

VIOLETTA. I think so.

CHRIS. I see what you get for being nice. Look at me. Freddy Krueger.

VIOLETTA. I don't think so. Look tough now. Like Mike Tyson. Good for a man to have some mark. Make him seem serious.

CHRIS. Ha.

VIOLETTA. True.

CHRIS. Whatever…

(Still, he checks himself out in the bowl's reflection.)

VIOLETTA. Chris… You don't have to hurt Nini… Okay? You call. Tell your father. I make some money. Two days, I pay you back. For both.

(**CHRIS** *scoffs.*)

VIOLETTA. I promise.

CHRIS. Yeah? How you gonna make a thousand bucks in two days, Violetta? If that's even your real name. You still think money falls from the trees up here?

VIOLETTA. No, but – I make it.

(*He looks at her.*)

CHRIS. What'd you do in TJ, huh? Tell me the truth.

VIOLETTA. Told you –

CHRIS. Work in a club, right?

VIOLETTA. Sí.

CHRIS. Doing what?

VIOLETTA. Dancing.

CHRIS. Ha.

VIOLETTA. Club pay me. They have people with camera, video us dancing, show it on the téles outside, make men come in, pay money.

CHRIS. And Nini?

VIOLETTA. Nini work outside, on corner. See some gringos, go to them with the postcards – "Hey amigos, you want see some putas? Come this way, man. Pretty girl, cheap cover…"

CHRIS. So he's your pimp, right? In a way…

(*Beat.*)

VIOLETTA. Chris. You tell me what to do, I do it. Por fa'… Please. I need help.

(*Long pause.*)

(*He doesn't say anything, just stares at her.*)

(*She gets up, moves the metal bowl out of the way, and kneels in front of him.*)

(*He watches her.*)

(*She starts to undo his belt.*)

CHRIS. What're you doing…?

VIOLETTA. Call your papá. Okay?

CHRIS. Come on –

VIOLETTA. Call him now.

CHRIS. Wait. Hold on a sec –

(She has his fly open.)

VIOLETTA. Please…

(He pushes her away.)

CHRIS. Stop it! Damn… What'd I say?

(Beat.)

Make me lose my temper and shit…

(He re-buckles his belt.)

(Long pause.)

VIOLETTA. Chris?

CHRIS. What?

VIOLETTA. You maricón?

CHRIS. What?

VIOLETTA. Like other men?

CHRIS. What? What are you talking about?

VIOLETTA. It's okay, if this is true. I just –

CHRIS. No! What – I ain't like that. Who said that?

VIOLETTA. What then?

CHRIS. Nothing! I just ain't no fucking rapist, all right?

VIOLETTA. Okay. Sorry. Sorry for this…

(Pause.)

CHRIS. You want to hear something stupid, Violetta? I mean real fucking stupid. This is gonna sound loco to you, probably. We known each other all of a couple days… And you hate me and everything, but –

VIOLETTA. I no hate you.

CHRIS. Okay.

VIOLETTA. I no hate –

CHRIS. Anyways. It doesn't matter, I just – You know what I was thinking? For a minute back there?

(VIOLETTA *shakes her head.*)

Thought I was in love with you.

(*Laughs.*)

You believe that? Love at first sight? You know what that
is?

VIOLETTA. Sí.

CHRIS. Swear to God. That's what I was thinking. When I
first saw you – Sitting by the wall over there. All barfing
and smelling like bananas. I was like, "Holy crap, you
know what? I think I might love that mojada over
there."

VIOLETTA. That is no love…

CHRIS. Sí. It is. I think so. It could be. Felt like I could
hear what you were thinking. Before I even found out
you could speak English, I was like, "She's hungry.
She's scared. That Mexican's a person, like me. We
understand each other…

(VIOLETTA *makes a sound.*)

You ever feel like that, Violetta? Connected to
someone…?

(*Beat.*)

VIOLETTA. Sí…

CHRIS. I'm not saying me, I'm just – Hey, you know what?
Don't even matter. I know how it was for me, that's all.

(*Pause.*)

Probably think I'm a pussy now, right?

VIOLETTA. No. I don't.

CHRIS. You know that word? "Pussy"?

VIOLETTA. Sí.

CHRIS. Of course you do…

(*They sit there.*)

VIOLETTA. Chris.

CHRIS. What?

VIOLETTA. Why you tell me all this?

CHRIS. I don't know. I'm a idiot, that's why.

VIOLETTA. What you want me to do?

CHRIS. Nothing. I'm not asking you for anything. I just...

VIOLETTA. Scared of your papá?

CHRIS. No, not that...

VIOLETTA. What then?

(**CHRIS** *shakes his head.*)

You help us? Please? Don't hurt Nini...

CHRIS. Then what?

VIOLETTA. Then...?

CHRIS. Then he comes back, right? Picks you up. And you two live happily ever after in America, ¿sí?

VIOLETTA. ¿Sí...?

CHRIS. And what about me, man? I'm stuck here. This is where I'm from. Where am I supposed to go?

VIOLETTA. You say you love me, Chris... It's not true?

(*Long pause.*)

(*He picks up the CB radio.*)

CHRIS. (*Re: himself.*) Stupid, man... Stupid.

(*He turns on the radio. Looks at* **VIOLETTA.**)

Roadrunner? Hey – You got your ears on?

(*Static.*)

Roadrunner? This is Wile E. I need your twenty.

VIOLETTA. (*Whispering.*) Chris?

CHRIS. What?

VIOLETTA. Gracias...

(*He shakes his head, looks away.*)

(**VIOLETTA** *sits down in a chair.*)

CHRIS. How 'bout ya, Roadrunner? Got your ears on? I need to talk...

Scene Nine

(The cab of the truck.)

*(**BILLY** drives. **NINI** next to him, tied up with cord.)*

(Outside, the desert at night.)

NINI. Hey, Billy, you know what funny?

(No response.)

I come to U.S. in back, man, under bananas, dripping on my face. Spiders... Tarantulas. Almost go crazy, with all that smell. But I go back to Mexico in front seat. First Class!

(No response.)

*(**NINI** looks around, scared.)*

Where you taking me, man?

(No response.)

Hey – Billy, you mind?

(He points to the radio, gets no response.)

(He reaches for the dash with his bound hands, fiddles with the dial.)

(A religious broadcast.)

(Talk radio.)

*(A ranchero tune. **NINI** leaves it, leans back in his seat.)*

*(**BILLY** glances over at him.)*

BILLY. *(Approving.)* Well, all right...

(They sit there for a moment, listening to the song.)

*(**BILLY** opens the glove box, takes out some no-doz in a blister pack.)*

NINI. Hey – You know what I like, Billy?

BILLY. What's that?

NINI. Crazy Horse, man.

BILLY. You a drinker?

NINI. What? No, the Indian –

BILLY. Right.

NINI. You don't know him, Billy?

BILLY. Not personally.

NINI. He native, like you, man. Me too. Part Azteca, on my mamma-half, know that? We real Norte Americanos. Have to stick together, no?

> *(Pause.)*

Serious. We here at the start, hermano, ¿verdad? Then los Españoles, los Ingleses come over in boats, take all our shit away, ¿sí? Conquistadores go home, white people come this time. Zachary Taylor. Ulysses S. Grant. Take all MY shit again, second chance. Pendejos draw a line. Try to make us against each other. But we the same, Billy. You and me...

BILLY. Don't know about that.

NINI. No?

> **(BILLY** *swallows the pills.)*

How come, man? You don't think so? I think so.

> *(Pause.)*

You know what I like about Crazy Horse, Billy? I tell you. He kill a whole bunch of white people with bow and arrow, man. I love to read about that shit in books. Love that...

BILLY. *(Amused.)* My daddy's white, you know.

NINI. Yeah, but you indio, Billy. Understand.

BILLY. Only half.

NINI. Ain't no half. White or color, no? Michael Jackson half. People still say he black.

BILLY. Michael Jackson was black.

NINI. That's what I saying, man.

BILLY. No, I mean – His parents were black. Both of 'em.

NINI. *(Incredulous.)* What?

BILLY. Yeah.

NINI. Not both.

BILLY. Sí.

NINI. How he got all –

> *(Gestures at his face.)*

– palido then, man? You sure?

BILLY. Positive. He did something to his skin.

NINI. Huh… I can't believe that, man. I don't think so.

> *(**NINI** sits back in his seat.)*
>
> *(Long pause.)*

You a good guy, Bill.

BILLY. Not really.

NINI. You could just drop me off, you know. In the desert here. You could do that. No one ever find out. I don't tell.

BILLY. Too late for that.

NINI. I'm scared, man…

> *(**BILLY** glances over at him.)*

BILLY. It's nothing personal.

NINI. Sí. I know that.

BILLY. We all gotta get by, right? Look after our own.

> *(**NINI** nods.)*

NINI. Sí. That's true.

> *(They both sit there, watching the headlights on the road.)*

What will happen to Violetta?

BILLY. She'll be all right.

NINI. What happen? Tell me, Bill. I need to know.

BILLY. Don't worry about it.

NINI. Don't sell her to no putería, Bill. I kill you.

BILLY. I told you don't worry.

NINI. I'm saying don't sell her. I come back from death and atormentar, man. Fucking fantasmo.

BILLY. Look. She'll stay at our place, all right? For a while. Do some cooking, cleaning. Earn her fee. And then… We'll let her go. Sound fair?

NINI. I don't believe you.

BILLY. I don't really give a shit what you believe. I told you what'll happen.

NINI . I know how you people are.

BILLY. You don't know shit. I'm married. Happily. Got no interest in your bony-butted piece, okay?

> *(Beat.)*

NINI. Hey, Billy, stop the truck a minute, man. I gotta cagar.

BILLY. Hold it in.

NINI. No, I gotta go now, man. My inside hurt.

BILLY. All of a sudden?

NINI. Yes, all a sudden! I scared! My stomach loose. Your American food make me hechar una firma, you know? KFC? Burger King? I don't want to shit up your vehicle, but…

BILLY. You dirty this cab, I'll fucking shoot you right now.

NINI. You shoot me anyways, no?

> *(Beat.)*

Come on. If you no gonna stop, man, do it now. Shoot my face. Get blood and brain all over your truck. I don't care. Or else let me go outside, and then kill me afterward, nice and clean, okay? Either way, you don't stop now, this puto camión be nasty, man. Have to happen.

BILLY. No way.

NINI. Come on, man! You ain't never had to shit bad? It's urgente! I'm telling you!

BILLY. We're almost there.

(Beat.)

NINI. All right, Billy, look. I have confession to make.

(**BILLY** *glances over at him.*)

BILLY. What?

NINI. I gotta make confession, man.

BILLY. I look like a priest to you?

NINI. Not that kind.

BILLY. I don't want to hear it.

NINI. Well, I tell you anyways. I got no grandma, Billy.

(Beat.)

BILLY. Whatever, man…

NINI. I tell you she working in U.S.? Cleaning motel? Not true. Not true.

BILLY. Fine. I forgive you.

NINI. No, I mean, yes, I have one, okay. Mi abuela. But she farm goat in Chiapas, man. Never been to U.S. before. Most money she ever see together in one place probably like twenty pesos… The truth, Billy? I come over working for the Zetas, man.

(**BILLY** *glances over at him.*)

BILLY. What are you talking about?

NINI. Got a medio kilo de la blanca stuffed up my ass right now.

(Pats his stomach.)

Fifteen thousand dólares, U.S. In my stomach. I'm fucking rich, Billy. Believe that?

BILLY. No.

NINI. Supposed to deliver in Phoenix. Get the fees. But I too nervous to shit until now. Be waiting, but it never come. That's why I got nothing for you, at first…

BILLY. *(To himself.)* You gotta be kidding me…

NINI. I hope I am, man, but no. Bad luck for us. They come looking, man. When I gone. That why I tell you now.

They know you bring me. They come looking, and I no around, they get sospechoso. They gonna be hurting people. I don't want them hurt Violetta…

>   *(Beat.)*

BILLY. I think you're lying.

NINI. ¿Sí? Untie me then. I shit right now and show you.

>   *(Beat.)*
>
>   *(The heavy sigh of the truck's hydraulic brakes.)*
>
>   *(The truck stops.)*
>
>   (**BILLY** *looks at* **NINI**.)

BILLY. You try to run, I'll go home and shoot her in the eye. Understand? Don't even dream about that.

NINI. I understand, sí. Where I do it then?

BILLY. Right here.

NINI. In the truck, man?

BILLY. On the seat. Where I can see.

NINI. You joking.

BILLY. I look like I'm joking?

>   (**NINI** *looks around.*)

NINI. For real, man?

BILLY. Sí. Right here.

NINI. Okay, but I ain't cleaning. Hear me? Ain't no empleada. You gringos do that for one time. Clean up after me for change.

>   (**BILLY** *reaches in the back, pulls out a spare plastic sheet, and spreads it out in the cab.*)
>
>   (*He takes the shotgun down from the rack and cradles it in his lap, pointed at* **NINI**.)
>
>   (*He unties* **NINI**'*s hands.*)

BILLY. You got thirty seconds.

NINI. You want to give me some privacy, man? You maricón or what?

(**BILLY** *snorts, looks away.*)

(**NINI** *unbuckles his belt as if to take down his pants.*)

(*He pulls the staple gun from where it's tucked in his waist, grabs* **BILLY**'s *forehead with his free hand, presses the stapler against* **BILLY**'s *throat, underneath his chin, and pulls the trigger.*)

(*There are three quick, dull snaps, and a spray of blood hits the windshield.*)

(**BILLY** *makes a strangling noise and kicks back against* **NINI**, *slamming him into the passenger-side window and splintering the safety glass.*)

(*Suddenly, the CB radio on the dashboard crackles to life.*)

CHRIS. (*Voice-over.*) Roadrunner? Hey – You got your ears on?

(**BILLY** *tries to reach for the radio.* **NINI** *grabs his arm and they struggle frantically, both of them gasping for air.*)

(**BILLY** *runs out of breath first. He claws at his stapled windpipe, his mouth opening and closing, and then he falls forward onto the steering wheel.*)

(*The blast of the truck horn drowns out everything for a few seconds.*)

(**NINI** *grabs* **BILLY**'s *head and props him up in the seat, cutting off the horn. He takes deep, gulping breaths of air.*)

CHRIS. (*Voice-over.*) Roadrunner? This is Wile E. Need your twenty...

Scene Ten

(The safe house.)

*(Static from the radio. **CHRIS** slaps it like it's broken.)*

CHRIS. Come on, Roadrunner. Wake up... Where the hell are you?

(More static.)

VIOLETTA. Ay, no...

*(**VIOLETTA** starts to break down. She sinks to the floor.)*

*(**CHRIS** kneels next to her.)*

CHRIS. Hey – Violetta? Look at me.

(She shivers silently, covering her face.)

*(**CHRIS** doesn't quite know what to do. He thinks about rubbing her back, smoothing her hair.)*

You want some coffee...? It's in the car. I'll put some Jack in it. Right? Make you feel better. Calm your nerves. I'm gonna have some. Have some, all right?

(He stands up.)

I'll be right back.

(Hesitates.)

I'm not gonna tie you, okay?

(Pause.)

Violetta? I'm not gonna tie you this time... While I'm gone. Just – stay here, all right? Please?

(She doesn't respond.)

Okay then...

(He exits.)

*(After a moment, **VIOLETTA** takes a deep, shuddering breath. She stands shakily, holding onto the desk for balance.)*

(*She looks around, catches sight of the hammer* **CHRIS** *left behind.*)

(*She picks it up, takes an experimental swing or two.*)

(*She puts it back down.*)

(*Instead, she goes to the mirror and looks at her reflection. She pinches her lips and cheeks, fixes her hair, tries to rub some of the swelling from her eyes.*)

(*She unbuttons the top button of her shirt and sits, arranging herself carefully on the floor as before.*)

(**CHRIS** *re-enters, carrying a thermos, a bottle of whiskey, and a couple styrofoam cups. He sees* **VIOLETTA**.)

CHRIS. Still here. Cool.

(*She looks up at him.*)

VIOLETTA. Where I have to go?

(*He puts the cups on the desk, pours the drinks.*)

CHRIS. (*Trying to joke.*) I don't know... Thought maybe you'd – Try to dig a tunnel under the wall, like *Shawshank* or something.

(*He offers her a cup.*)

Here you go. Got some kick to it.

(*Shows a bottle.*)

Black Label. You'll feel better.

(*She takes the cup.*)

VIOLETTA. Chris?

CHRIS. ¿Sí?

VIOLETTA. You want to marry me?

(*He looks up.*)

CHRIS. Say what?

VIOLETTA. Marry to me? You want this?

(*Beat.*)

CHRIS. Fuck you, man.

VIOLETTA. What?

CHRIS. See? I was being serious back there… Don't make fun of that.

VIOLETTA. I am not. I am being serious. You say you love me, no? But you don't want to?

CHRIS. Come on – What are you talking about?

VIOLETTA. Not this kind of love, ¿sí? I understand.

CHRIS. No, that's – I want to, yeah. I want to. I just – Where's all this coming from?

VIOLETTA. Your father say he sell me.

CHRIS. Oh. He was just – Don't worry about that. He won't – I wouldn't let him.

VIOLETTA. I am scared…

CHRIS. Hey, listen. I won't let anything happen to you, all right? Ever. I promise.

VIOLETTA. You marry me then? ¿Sí?

> *(Beat.)*

CHRIS. 'Cause you need the ID, right? The green card? The – card verde? Is that why –

VIOLETTA. Part of this, but –

CHRIS. And we'd be friends or something, like –

VIOLETTA. Friends?

CHRIS. I mean – You'd just want to be – Just to be straight up, you'd want to have conversations or something. Not like –

VIOLETTA. "Friends," I no –

CHRIS. Like brother and sister.

VIOLETTA. Sorry. I no understand. My English –

CHRIS. If we got married, Violetta, you wouldn't want to do it for real, right? Just the –

VIOLETTA. You mean sex thing?

> *(He laughs, embarrassed.)*

CHRIS. Nah, I just – I don't know what the hell I mean. I'm just – surprised is all.

VIOLETTA. We can do this too, Chris, if you want – Husband and wife.

CHRIS. You would want to?

VIOLETTA. Sí. If we are married.

(*He looks at her, laughs.*)

CHRIS. My pop would fucking murder me...

VIOLETTA. We do it now then, ¿sí? Before he come home. The place open?

CHRIS. City Hall?

VIOLETTA. Mm?

CHRIS. Yeah, probably. On a Monday? I guess.

(*She takes his hand, kisses him.*)

(*He pulls away. Looks for something to do.*)

Cool. Okay. Yeah. So... My ma might have something you could wear. If you wanted to like – Dress up a little first?

VIOLETTA. Okay.

CHRIS. You can clean up a bit. If you want. I mean you look fine now, but –

VIOLETTA. I clean up.

(*He looks at her, brushes her hair out of her face.*)

CHRIS. Violetta?

VIOLETTA. ¿Sí?

CHRIS. I got blood all over you.

VIOLETTA. It's okay.

CHRIS. Looks good on you though... Like a girl ninja, you know? Ever heard that word before? "Ninja"?

VIOLETTA. No.

CHRIS. Ha. It's Japanese. See?

(*Taps his temple.*)

I finally got you...

Scene Eleven

(The safe house. Later.)

(The room is empty.)

(Suddenly, a loud pounding at the door.)

*(The door is kicked open, and **NINI** enters, his face spattered with blood, holding **BILLY**'s shotgun.)*

NINI. ¿Violeta? ¿Estás aquí? Soy yo… ¿Dónde?

(He glances around, peeks into the back room, comes out.)

*(He picks up **VIOLETTA**'s floral-print dress, looks at it.)*

Scene Twelve

(**NINI** *paces, the shotgun in his hand. He checks his watch.*)

(*He picks up the snow globe he gave* **VIOLETTA**, *looks at it.*)

(*The sound of a car pulling up outside.*)

(**NINI** *puts the globe back on the desk and ducks behind the plastic sheeting just as the front door opens and* **CHRIS** *enters, leading* **VIOLETTA**.)

(*She wears a light-colored dress, much too big for her, secured with a man's silk tie around her waist.* **CHRIS** *has on a suit, cowboy boots, and a bolo.*)

(*They both wear cheap silver rings from a pawnshop.*)

CHRIS. Pop? You home? We got a announcement!

(**VIOLETTA** *glances at the globe, sees the snow still settling.*)

(*She looks around.*)

Pop...? You home? You're not gonna believe this, but –

NINI. Don't fucking move, pinche gringo.

(**CHRIS** *freezes.*)

Stay there. Don't turn round.

(**NINI** *comes out from behind the plastic, holding the shotgun level at* **CHRIS**' *chest.*)

VIOLETTA. Ninito – ¿Estás bien?

NINI. Tranquilo. Apúrate. Anda y busca tu maleta.

(**VIOLETTA** *goes to him, touches his face, as though she can't believe he's real.*)

Come on – Tenemos que apurarnos.

VIOLETTA. ¿Qué te pasó, Nini?

NINI. Luego lo conversamos. Agarra la maldita maleta –

CHRIS. What happened? Where's Billy?

(**NINI** *points the gun at him.*)

NINI. Shut up! Shut the fuck up, white boy! Nobody here talking to you!

VIOLETTA. Ninito –

NINI. Eh?

VIOLETTA. ¿Por qué estas sangrado?

NINI. No te preocupes.

VIOLETTA. Está muerto…?

NINI. ¡Violetta! Venga, nena… We talk about this later on, okay? Hurry now!

CHRIS. What happened? Where is he?

VIOLETTA. ¿Nini? ¿La policia te está persiguiendo?

CHRIS. *(Panicked.)* Where'd he go? What's happening? Somebody speak fucking English!

> *(**CHRIS** takes a step toward **NINI**, and **NINI** pumps the shotgun.)*

NINI. Ah-ah.

> *(**CHRIS** hesitates, looks around for something to fight with.)*

> *(To **VIOLETTA**.)*

Ya estubo, muchacha. Vámanos! People be asking for him on the radio now. Got no time…

> *(**VIOLETTA** looks at **CHRIS**, back at **NINI**.)*

Come on!

VIOLETTA. No voy contigo, Ninito.

NINI. ¿Qué?

VIOLETTA. No voy contigo.

NINI. What you talking about, girl?

VIOLETTA. I can no… Not now. Sorry…

> *(Beat.)*

> *(**NINI** looks at **CHRIS**.)*

NINI. What happen?

CHRIS. We got married, man.

> *(Showing his ring.)*

CHRIS. See?

NINI. We? Who got?

> *(Beat.)*

Married? ¿De qué chingados me hablas?

VIOLETTA. No sabía que más hacer. Pensé que estabas muerto!

> *(Beat.)*

NINI. Bueno… Don't matter. Nobody know. We go back home, eh? Forget all about this. Get married for real –

VIOLETTA. And do what?

NINI. Live! What you think?

VIOLETTA. Live? Pinche border trash? ¿Migrantes del tercer mundo?

NINI. So? We be together…

> *(Beat.)*

VIOLETTA. *(Shakes her head, sadly.)* Better for you down there, Ninito… Un nacionalista. Un Republicano. Not me. Not me…

NINI. ¿Ya no me amas eh?

> **(VIOLETTA** *shakes her head.)*
>
> *(Beat.)*

NINI. ¿Y nuestro bebe?

VIOLETTA. No es tu bebe, Nini.

NINI. ¿Cómo?

VIOLETTA. No es tuyo.

NINI. Mierda.

VIOLETTA. It's verdad.

> *(Beat.)*
>
> **(NINI** *slowly turns toward* **CHRIS.***)*

NINI. You tell him that? That bullshit what you tell him?

CHRIS. *(Doesn't know what they're talking about.)* Yeah, she told me, man. I know all about it, yeah.

(**NINI** *raises the gun, points it at* **CHRIS**.)

NINI. Ey – You think you something, huh? You special, right?

CHRIS. No...

VIOLETTA. Ninito –

NINI. You think something about you... Huh? But she doing this only for Green Card, cabrón. That's all. So the baby be born here, in U.S. Nothing about you. Okay? You ain't even person to her. Just fucking passaporte!

CHRIS. I know that.

> (**NINI** *presses the gun into* **CHRIS**' *face, hard enough to leave a mark.*)

NINI. She don't love you, guey! Hear me? Understand. Born fifty miles down from here, on other side, you just like me. A bag of shit! Un menos que humano!

> (**CHRIS** *nods.*)
>
> (*Beat.*)

VIOLETTA. Ninito... Go home, eh? You still make it across, if you run.

> (**NINI** *hesitates, struggling.*)
>
> (*Suddenly, he grabs the snow globe off the desk and hurls it against the wall.*)
>
> (*The glass ball shatters and the snow/glitter explodes all over the room.*)
>
> (**NINI** *turns and stumbles to the door, runs outside.*)
>
> (*The sound of the truck starting up, grinding its gears and pulling away.*)
>
> (**VIOLETTA** *takes a deep breath, steadying herself.*)
>
> (*After a moment:*)

VIOLETTA. Lo siento, Christopher...

CHRIS. It's all right.

VIOLETTA. Sorry I don't tell you before. About this baby.

CHRIS. It's okay. I knew about it.

(*She looks at him.*)

VIOLETTA. ¿Cómo…?

CHRIS. I ain't stupid. I know stuff. Don't matter, all right? Not to me. I'm happy about it.

VIOLETTA. ¿Verdad?

CHRIS. Sí. It's all right.

VIOLETTA. Okay. Gracias…

(*She starts to clean the broken globe off the floor.*)

CHRIS. Hey – What'd he say about my pop, Violetta? What happen to –

VIOLETTA. Oh, they get in fight. On border. Nini hit him. Knock him down. But I think – he come home soon, Chris. Not to worry about this, okay?

CHRIS. (*He knows she's lying.*) Okay… Good to know…

VIOLETTA. Chris – I'm sorry he say those things to you.

CHRIS. Not your fault.

VIOLETTA. I think you are nice. More than passaporte.

CHRIS. Yeah.

VIOLETTA. We family now, eh?

CHRIS. Yeah. I guess so. I guess we are.

(*Beat.*)

Can I ask you something else, Violetta?

VIOLETTA. Sí. Of course. What?

CHRIS. What'd you tell him there? To make him go?

VIOLETTA. I tell him we marry now. Oficial.

CHRIS. No no, but – Something else? Something – about this baby?

VIOLETTA. Oh. I tell him he is not the papá of this one.

CHRIS. Yeah. Is that true?

(*She shakes her head slightly, continues cleaning.*)

CHRIS. Good. 'Cause I always liked the guy, you know? Before he smashed my face and everything... He seemed nice.

(She nods.)

VIOLETTA. Hey – You hungry now, Chris?

CHRIS. Not really.

VIOLETTA. I am hungry. I am always hungry.

CHRIS. Probably sick of Rice-A-Ronis though, right? Sorry. I can't make nothing else.

VIOLETTA. It's okay. I make. What you want? ¿Hamburguesas? Cheeseburgers?

CHRIS. Yeah. Is that okay for you?

VIOLETTA. Yes. I like them too.

CHRIS. Okay... Yeah. Sounds great. Gracias.

(She opens the cupboards, takes down some food, and turns on the hot plate.)

(He turns on the radio. Music starts to play. A ranchero tune.)

(He sits at the table, stares off into space.)

(As she starts to cook the meat on the hot plate, the lights fade.)

End of Play